CANADA

Minnesota

Wisconsin

Michigan

Iowa

Illinois   Indiana   Ohio

Missouri   Kentucky   West Virginia   Virginia

Oklahoma   Arkansas   Tennessee   North Carolina

Mississippi   Alabama   Georgia   South Carolina

Louisiana

Florida

New York

Pennsylvania

Massachusetts
Rhode Island
Connecticut
New Jersey
Delaware
Maryland
Washington, D.C.

N
W   E
S

The Twelve Days of Christmas in California

written and illustrated by
Laura Rader

STERLING

New York / London

Dear Brad,

Happy holidays to my favorite cousin!

It's sunny and seventy degrees here in southern California. We are all having a great Christmas vacation and we can't wait for you to get here—awesome adventures await you! There's so much to see and do, so we're going to celebrate the twelve days of Christmas on beaches, in the desert, in the mountains, and in the forests. You might want to bring your hiking boots _and_ your sandals, your sunglasses _and_ your down jacket, just to be safe. From celebrities strolling around Hollywood to redwood trees towering over hikers in Yosemite National Park, our state has **EVERYTHING!**

Lots of people "rushed" to California in 1848 to find gold. But there are so many other golden things to discover here. You'll see that it's not called the Golden State for nothing.

Hurry! Hurry! I can't wait to see you.

'Bye for now!

Your cousin,

Teri

Dear Mom and Dad,

Here I am in sunny California! Cousin Teri, Uncle Bo, and Aunt Dora met me at the San Diego airport with a very special gift—a little quail sitting on top of a miniature redwood tree! The redwood is California's state tree and the California valley quail is the state bird. I named her "Cali." She's super smart.

We drove along the harbor of San Diego and saw the huge U.S. Navy ships. I imagined the Spanish explorers sailing into these same waters almost 500 years ago. Uncle Bo knows all about California history, and he told me that in 1542, Juan Rodríguez Cabrillo first sailed into an uncharted bay area and noted it in his explorer's log. Many years later, another explorer from Spain, Sebastian Vizcaino, arrived in his ship, the San Diego, and decided to name the bay area after it. The San Diego Bay was born!

Teri says that the California shoreline is different everywhere you go— up north it's sometimes bordered by sharp cliffs, but here it's covered in soft, warm sand, perfect for surfers, swimmers, and dolphins.

Uncle Bo bought us a lunch I've definitely never tried before— FISH tacos! Cali thought they were delicious, too.

Love, Brad

Dear Mom and Dad,

This morning we packed up the car for our California adventure. Aunt Dora says that we have a LOT of ground to cover—California takes up over half of the West Coast! I feel like an explorer and I know I'm in for lots of exciting discoveries.

Everyone knows about the San Diego Zoo and the incredible aquarium at SeaWorld (wow!), but there are amazing animals EVERYWHERE you look. Today as we started our trip up along the coast, we saw two gray whales (California's state marine mammals) making their own journey. These giants swim from Alaska all the way down to the warm Baja lagoons—the one and only place where they give birth to their calves.

Our next stop was the famous Mission San Juan Capistrano, nicknamed "The Mission of the Swallows" and founded in 1776 by a Spanish priest named Junípero Serra who wanted to offer a safe "rest stop" for travelers. I had hoped to see the swallows but they won't return until March. Bummer.

Love, Brad

CALI'S FACTS
Every year, gray whales swim 12,500 miles from the Arctic waters above Alaska to Baja, California!

Dear Mom and Dad,

Today we set up camp—in the DESERT! We are in Joshua Tree National Park and I've already seen some crazy sights. Uncle Bo and Teri led the way on a hike. I got my first glimpse of a Joshua tree, with its weird, spiky arms pointing in every direction. We also saw lots of little desert critters scurrying around. There were geckos, iguanas, some snakes, and a very shy tarantula. Cali found a whole bunch of friends here, too. There are at least 250 kinds of birds that live in the California desert.

Teri was very excited to show me three cute and prickly "hedgehogs"—a kind of cactus. There are lots of other cacti with funny names, too, like "beavertails," "bunny ears," and "teddy bears."

Have you ever heard of "star parties"? No, we're not in Hollywood yet! Since there are no other lights around, you can see REAL stars SUPER clearly in the desert night sky—even the Milky Way! We all ooh-ed and ah-ed along with other stargazers. It was really something.

Love, Brad

CALI'S FACTS
"Teddy Bear" is the cute nickname for a fuzzy-looking cholla cactus.

CALI'S FACTS
Hummingbirds are the
only birds known to fly
BACKWARD!

Dear Mom and Dad,

Remember watching the Tournament of Roses parade on TV last year? Well here I am in Pasadena—and the whole town is setting up for this year's parade! Millions of flowers will be used to decorate the incredible floats. Aunt Dora says that the first parade was held in 1890 when people who used to live in snowy climates wanted to show friends back home the blooming flowers of Southern California.

Aunt Dora was excited to show me the Huntington Botanical Gardens in nearby San Marino, too. There are more than 15,000 different kinds of plants there, including one of the world's largest collections of cacti. Teri and I couldn't believe how BIG some of them were—they looked like aliens from another planet!

In another part of the garden, I found a bush with lots of red flowers. It sounded like it was humming. Then I saw four of the tiniest birds zipping around it—HUMMINGBIRDS! Their tiny wings beat so fast that they "hummed," and their feathers sparkled like green and purple jewels.

We left the hummers in peace to eat their nectar lunch, and went out for cheeseburgers. Uncle Bo says they were invented right here in Pasadena in 1920! (Teri ordered a veggie burger, and so did Cali.)

Love, Brad

On the fourth day of Christmas,
my cousin gave to me . . .

4 hummingbirds

3 hedgehogs, 2 spouting whales,
and a quail in a redwood tree.

HOLLYWOOD

Mann's Chinese Theater

Griffith Observatory

George C. Page Museum La Brea Tar Pits

Hollywood Bowl

Dear Mom and Dad,

Hello from Hollywood!! Did you know that there are more than 2,000 stars on the Walk of Fame? We saw loads of famous names, from musicians to movie directors to actors to cartoon characters! Teri joked that all five of us (Cali, too) should have our own stars here.

Outside Grauman's Chinese Theatre, lots of famous people have pressed their hand- and footprints into the cement sidewalk. You'd be surprised by how many actors have really big feet!

When we toured the Kodak Theatre, the home of the Academy Awards, I presented Teri with the Oscar for being the coolest cousin. She totally deserved it.

From there we drove to the gooey La Brea Tar Pits. Fossils from 28,000 years ago have been pulled out in almost perfect condition. We even got to see the state fossil—the sabre-toothed cat. One look at its 8-inch long teeth gave me goosebumps!

The Griffith Observatory (perfect for looking at far-away planets) and the Hollywood Bowl (a HUGE performance amphitheatre) are two other places in Los Angeles where the "stars" come out. I'll have stars in my eyes for weeks!

Love, Brad

CALI'S FACTS
The letters in the giant Hollywood sign are 30 feet wide and 50 feet tall!

On the fifth day of Christmas,
my cousin gave to me . . .

5 shining stars

4 hummingbirds, 3 hedgehogs,
2 spouting whales,
and a quail in a redwood tree.

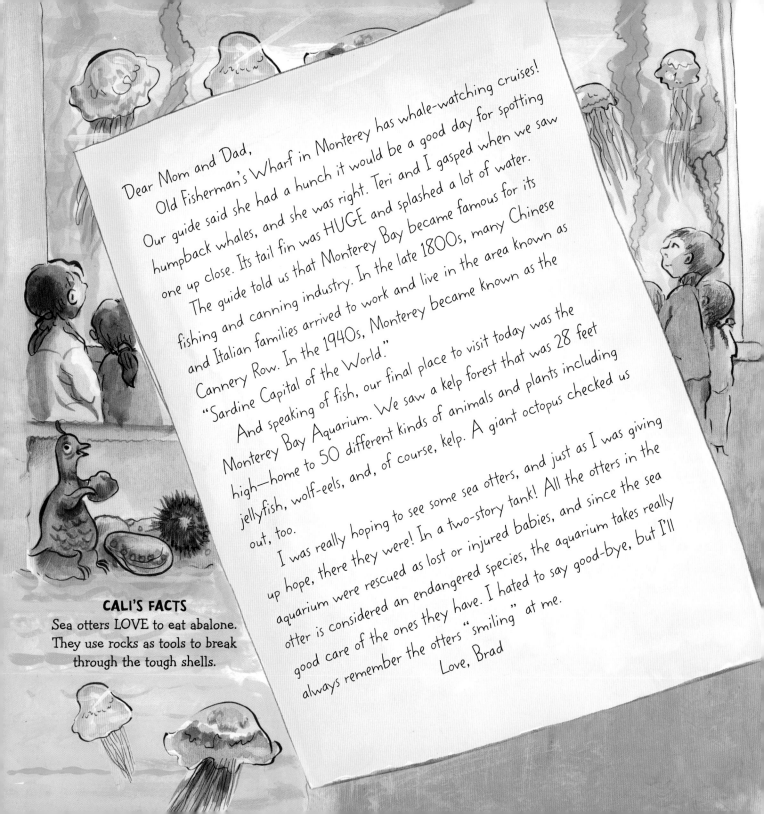

Dear Mom and Dad,

Old Fisherman's Wharf in Monterey has whale-watching cruises! Our guide said she had a hunch it would be a good day for spotting humpback whales, and she was right. Teri and I gasped when we saw one up close. Its tail fin was HUGE and splashed a lot of water.

The guide told us that Monterey Bay became famous for its fishing and canning industry. In the late 1800s, many Chinese and Italian families arrived to work and live in the area known as Cannery Row. In the 1940s, Monterey became known as the "Sardine Capital of the World."

And speaking of fish, our final place to visit today was the Monterey Bay Aquarium. We saw a kelp forest that was 28 feet high—home to 50 different kinds of animals and plants including jellyfish, wolf-eels, and, of course, kelp. A giant octopus checked us out, too.

I was really hoping to see some sea otters, and just as I was giving up hope, there they were! In a two-story tank! All the otters in the aquarium were rescued as lost or injured babies, and since the sea otter is considered an endangered species, the aquarium takes really good care of the ones they have. I hated to say good-bye, but I'll always remember the otters "smiling" at me.

Love, Brad

CALI'S FACTS
Sea otters LOVE to eat abalone. They use rocks as tools to break through the tough shells.

Dear Mom and Dad,

Hang ten! Wipe out! Cowabunga!! California beaches offer some of the best places to surf in the world. It was exciting to watch surfers riding gigantic waves--how do they stay on those boards?? Uncle Bo says he used to be pretty good on a surfboard, but he was nothing compared to a guy named George Freeth—the world's first professional surfer. George was born in 1883 in Hawaii, and started surfing when he was just a kid. In 1907, Jack London, the writer and adventurer, decided to write about him and the sport of surfing. Henry Huntington (the Huntington Gardens are named for him) read the story about George and invited him to come to Redondo Beach to demonstrate his skills. He inspired many future surfers with his gnarly moves on the waves!

I forgot to mention in my letter yesterday that we stopped for a tour of Hearst Castle in San Simeon. You would have loved it! William Randolph Hearst, a super rich newspaper publisher, built this place in 1867. Movie stars and famous people like Winston Churchill and Franklin D. Roosevelt stayed there. With 56 bedrooms and 61 bathrooms, there was plenty of space for guests. In the old days there was even a ZOO that had wild animals, including tigers! Roar!

Love, Brad

CALI'S FACTS

"Gnarly," "dude," and "wipe out" are a few words that originated with surfers. "Ripping" means to make daring, creative moves on a wave.

Dear Mom and Dad,

We have driven through miles and miles of farmland today. The entire country eats fruits and vegetables grown here—from artichokes to zucchini. The Central Valley is the world's largest agricultural area, but get this: it has no natural source of water! Water is brought into the area from the north through a wide concrete channel called the California Aqueduct. It's 443 miles long—wow!

Many of the world's "food capitals" are located here. Fresno is the raisin capital and Castroville is the artichoke capital. Gilroy is the garlic capital, and every year they have a garlic festival where there are contests to find the weirdest ways to use garlic—even in ice cream!!!

Farmers were giving out all kinds of free samples at the farmers' market we wandered through: almonds, raisins, artichokes, dates, walnuts, apples, oranges, and CACTUS CANDY! I never would have believed that the fruit of the prickly pear cactus could taste so sweet and delicious.

Aunt Dora bought us some toasted pepitas (pumpkin seeds) to munch on as we head for our next stop.

Love, Brad

You look familiar!

CALI'S FACTS
There are nearly 500 different varieties of avocados! San Diego County is the avocado capital of the USA.

NATURAL ORGANIC SOAPS & Lotions

On the eighth day of Christmas,
my cousin gave to me . . .

8 farmers selling

almonds

apples

cactus candy

oranges

walnuts

raisins

dates

artichokes

7 surfers ripping, 6 otters smiling,
5 shining stars, 4 hummingbirds,
3 hedgehogs, 2 spouting whales,
and a quail in a redwood tree.

CALI'S FACTS
The jagged peaks, domes, and canyons in Yosemite were formed by the grinding and shifting of ancient glaciers.

Dear Mom and Dad,

Now I know why Teri told me to pack my parka! We counted nine super-tall mountain peaks as we faced the Sierra Nevada range here in incredible Yosemite National Park. We saw waterfalls (frozen solid!) and big stretches of snowy meadows, too. We can enjoy this awesome place mostly because of a nature lover named John Muir, who dedicated his life to the conservation of wild places. In 1903, he asked President Theodore Roosevelt to help his cause. They camped out together at Glacier Point and the president was convinced that the natural wonders of Yosemite should be preserved. John Muir is known as the father of America's National Parks System. He was also the founder of the Sierra Club. Without him, this whole beautiful area could have highways and houses built all over it!

We went on a long hike and by the end we <u>still</u> had only seen a tiny bit of the 1,200 square mile park. It's the size of the state of Rhode Island! Black bears, bighorn sheep, and mountain lions live here. Not to be a chicken or anything, but I'm glad we didn't see any of them today. I would have been too tired to run away!

Love, Brad

On the ninth day of Christmas,
my cousin gave to me . . .

9 mountains rising

8 farmers selling, 7 surfers ripping,
6 otters smiling, 5 shining stars,
4 hummingbirds, 3 hedgehogs, 2 spouting whales,
and a quail in a redwood tree.

Dear Mom and Dad,

California sure is the Golden State! Golden poppies, golden stars, the Gold Rush, and now here we are at the Golden Gate Bridge, finished in 1937 by Joseph B. Strauss. Over a mile long, it connects San Francisco to Marin County. We took a cruise around San Francisco Bay, and going under the enormous bridge was so cool! We also got to see spooky Alcatraz Island (where gangster Al Capone spent his prison days), Angel Island, and Coit Tower.

As our cruise boat pulled into shore, the sea lions sunbathing nearby "barked" a big hello. Our boat had to pull in very slowly to avoid hurting any other sea lions that might be swimming in the water.

Oh, here's a name you might recognize: In 1853, another famous Strauss—Levi Strauss—arrived in San Francisco from New York. The 24-year-old Bavarian immigrant was the inventor of BLUE JEANS! The story goes that when the fabric worker arrived at the height of the Gold Rush, a miner suggested that Strauss make some sturdy pants for hard work. The first version wasn't very comfortable—too stiff! Then Strauss came up with the classic denim and riveted pocket system. He certainly found "gold" in his historic invention.

Love, Brad

CALI'S FACTS
Sea lions live all along California's coast. They're speedy swimmers and eat LOTS of fish. Their honking "barks" can get very loud—especially when they gather in groups.

Dear Mom and Dad,

Just as the miners needed tough work pants to wear, they also needed food to eat. San Francisco's Fisherman's Wharf began as a fish market during the Gold Rush of 1849, when miners—called "Forty-niners"—crowded into the area to hunt for gold. Last night we pretended to be hungry miners ourselves, and ate a seafood feast at the wharf—including Dungeness crab, a specialty here.

Andrew Smith Hallidie was a Scottish immigrant who came to California to find gold, but found something else instead: he invented San Francisco's famous cable car system. The hills here are unbelievably steep, and in 1869 Hallidie witnessed a horrible accident. Horses pulling a heavy wagon up a hill stumbled and crashed down the hill. Hallidie, an engineer, decided the city needed a better transportation solution. He and his supporters were ready in 1873 to run the first cable car. Lots of people laughed at the idea, but here we are today, riding in Hallidie's successful invention that changed San Francisco! There are about 40 brightly-painted cable cars in use. Their shiny brass bells can be heard clanging as the cars go up and down the crazy hills.

Love, Brad

CALI'S FACTS
A contest in Union Park honors the best cable car bell-ringer of the year!

Chinatown

Cable Car Museum

POWELL STREET

Fisherman's Wharf

On the eleventh day of Christmas, my cousin gave to me . . .

11 cable cars clanging

10 sea lions sunning, **9** mountains rising,
8 farmers selling, **7** surfers ripping, **6** otters smiling,
5 shining stars, **4** hummingbirds, **3** hedgehogs,
2 spouting whales, and a quail in a redwood tree.

Dear Mom and Dad,

Today we drove through a TREE! I am not kidding. There's a giant redwood tree you can drive right through—I have a photo to prove it. "Avenue of the Giants" is a 31-mile drive in Humboldt Redwoods State Park, with all kinds of tourist attractions and places to stop. When you stand under the giant trees, you feel like an ant. I will never forget looking up, up, up at the redwoods' branches swaying high above me.

The forests here in northern California are home to the tallest trees on Earth. In 2006, a new "world's tallest tree" was discovered here, near Eureka. It's a redwood named "Hyperion" that is 379 feet tall—six stories taller than the Statue of Liberty!

"Eureka" is a pretty funny name for a town, so I asked Aunt Dora about it. She told me that it was founded in 1850, during the Gold Rush. Back then, when gold miners would find a treasure, they would shout out "Eureka!" which is Greek for "I found it!" From 1848 to 1869, the search produced almost $250,000,000 in gold. People of all cultures settled here. Teri says that's why California is such an awesome state with so much variety. This has been the best vacation ever. Can I come back this summer?

Love, Brad

DRIVE
THRU
TREE

CALI'S FACTS
Redwoods take 400-500 years to reach maturity, and some have been growing for more than 2,000 years.

California: The Golden State

Capital: Sacramento · **State abbreviation:** CA · **State bird:** the California valley quail · **State flower:** the golden or California poppy · **State tree:** the California redwood · **State animal:** the grizzly bear · **State fish:** the golden trout · **State fossil:** the sabre-toothed cat · **State mineral:** gold · **State insect:** the California dogface butterfly · **State motto:** "Eureka!" ("I have found it!")

Some Famous Californians:

Maya Angelou (1928–) is an award-winning author and poet. While still in high school in San Francisco, she became the city's first female African-American streetcar conductor. She has written six autobiographies, including *I Know Why the Caged Bird Sings*.

Leonardo DiCaprio (1974–) is an Academy-Award®–nominated actor. A Los Angeles native, DiCaprio has starred in such popular films as *Titanic,* and is a devoted environmentalist.

Joe DiMaggio (1914–1999) was born in Martinez. He played baseball for the New York Yankees his entire fifteen-year career, from 1936 until 1951. His 56-game hitting streak remains unbeaten.

Walt Disney (1901–1966) co-founded what is now known as The Walt Disney Company with his brother, Roy. He helped create Mickey Mouse and provided the famous mouse's voice.

Isadora Duncan (1877–1927) is considered by many to be the mother of modern dance. Born in San Francisco, her career flourished in Europe. Her flowing scarves and barefoot performances were wildly different from the more rigid ballet of the time.

John Steinbeck (1902–1968), an author born in Salinas Valley, wrote many stories set in real California locales. The sea otters at the Monterey Bay Aquarium are named after characters from his novels, including *Cannery Row* and *The Grapes of Wrath*.

Mariano Vallejo (1807–1890) was born in Monterey when California was still part of Mexico. When the land was ceded to the U.S., Vallejo became a member of the first session of the new state's Senate. The city of Vallejo is named for him.

Venus (1980–) and **Serena Williams** (1981–) grew up in Compton and became extremely successful tennis players. The sisters have a total of five Olympic gold medals.

To my California friends, who have made me feel
welcome in their awesome state,
with love and gratitude.
—L.R.

STERLING and the distinctive Sterling logo are
registered trademarks of Sterling Publishing Co,. Inc

Library of Congress Cataloging-in-Publication Data Available

2 4 6 8 10 9 7 5 3 1
6/09

Published by Sterling Publishing Co., Inc.
387 Park Avenue South, New York, NY 10016
Text and illustrations copyright © 2009 by Laura Rader
The original illustrations for this book were created using inks and acrylic paints on Strathmore bristol vellum.
Designed by Kate Moll and Patrice Sheridan.
Distributed in Canada by Sterling Publishing
c/o Canadian Manda Group, 165 Dufferin Street
Toronto, Ontario, Canada M6K 3H6
Distributed in the United Kingdom by GMC Distribution Services
Castle Place, 166 High Street, Lewes, East Sussex, England BN7 1XU
Distributed in Australia by Capricorn Link (Australia) Pty. Ltd.
P.O. Box 704, Windsor, NSW 2756, Australia

Printed in China
All rights reserved

Sterling ISBN 978-1-4027-6247-5

For information about custom editions, special sales, premium and
corporate purchases, please contact Sterling Special Sales
Department at 800-805-5489 or specialsales@sterlingpublishing.com.

Washington

Oregon

Idaho

Montana

North
Dakota

South
Dakota

Wyoming

Nevada

Nebraska

Utah

Colorado

Kansas

California

New Mexico

Arizona

Hawaii

Texas

Alaska

MEXICO